The Notebooks of Lazarus Long

Robert A. Heinlein & D. F. Vassallo

G. P. PUTNAM'S SONS , NEW YORK

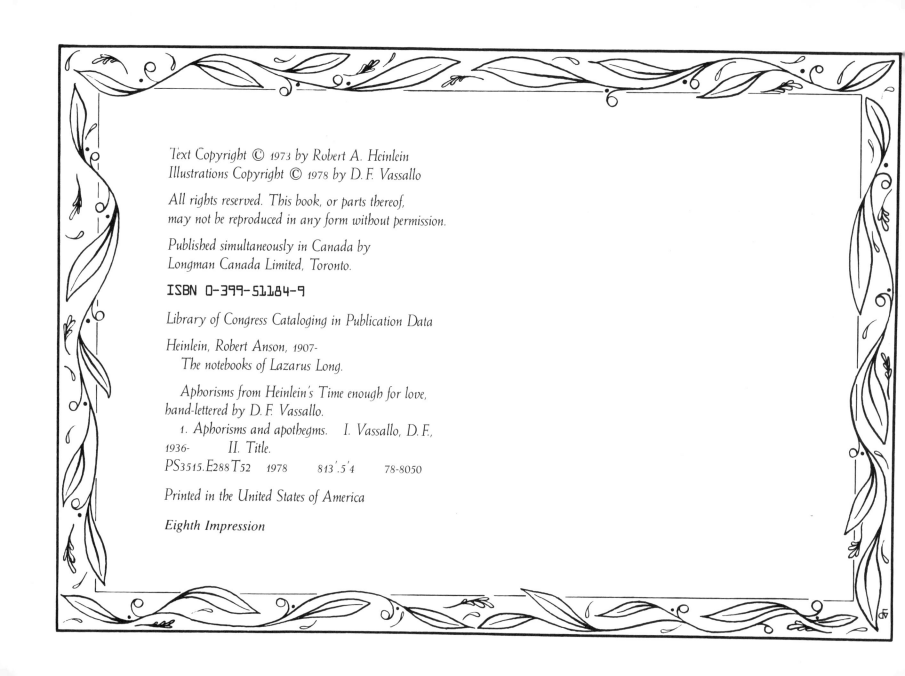

Published simultaneously in Canada by
Longman Canada Limited, Toronto.

ISBN 0-399-51184-9

Library of Congress Cataloging in Publication Data

Heinlein, Robert Anson, 1907-
    The notebooks of Lazarus Long.

    Aphorisms from Heinlein's Time enough for love,
hand-lettered by D. F. Vassallo.
    1. Aphorisms and apothegms.   I. Vassallo, D. F.,
1936-   II. Title.
PS3515.E288T52   1978   813'.5'4   78-8050

Printed in the United States of America

Eighth Impression

Introduction to the Notebooks of Lazarus Long.

Of all the memorable characters created in the works of Robert A. Heinlein, Lazarus Long, the immortal, stands out beyond the rest. Lazarus first appeared in <u>Methuselah's Children</u> in 1941, the central character of that novel which helped to establish the Golden Age of science fiction in <u>Astounding</u> magazine, and to establish Heinlein's future history series as a pinnacle of achievement in science fiction down to the present. But Heinlein's fans had to wait thirty years, until the publication of <u>Time Enough for Love</u>, for Lazarus to return to center stage.

Heinlein's future history, the massive series of stories and novels collected in <u>The Past Through Tomorrow</u> and <u>Orphans of the Sky</u>, was not completed until the appearance of <u>Time Enough for Love</u>, the longest and most highly developed of all Heinlein's novels, in which Lazarus Long, the oldest living member of the human race, lives and travels through time and space and unifies the great series.

Lazarus will never die. Humanity's dream of immortality is embodied in this wily lovable character who is, most of all, wise. His experience, over the thousands of years of his life, his continued zest for life, his ironic appreciation of the successes and failures of human society make his observations in his notebooks, originally published as interludes in Heinlein's huge novel of eternal life, essential reading. And the notebooks of Lazarus Long are entertaining. From the smallest details of daily life to overarching abstractions on the nature of the human condition, Lazarus' comments are acute, lively and intelligent.

So here are <u>The Notebooks of Lazarus Long</u> (alias Woodrow Wilson Smith; Mr. Justice Lenox; Corporal Ted Bronson; Proscribed Prisoner No. 83M2742; His Serenity Seraphin Above; et al., ad infinitum)—oldest living member of the human race by virtue of a unique set of chromosomes, clonal and other rejuvenation techniques, and a finely tuned sense of rational self-interest —who has pioneered eight planets, survived at least one lynch mob and many wives, fought in fifteen interstellar wars, made and lost numerous fortunes, and fathered a progeny which numbers in the billions. Lazarus' observations are illuminated for your delight by the noted calligrapher D.F. Vassallo. Read them for sheer enjoyment or to ponder their didactic message.

David G. Hartwell

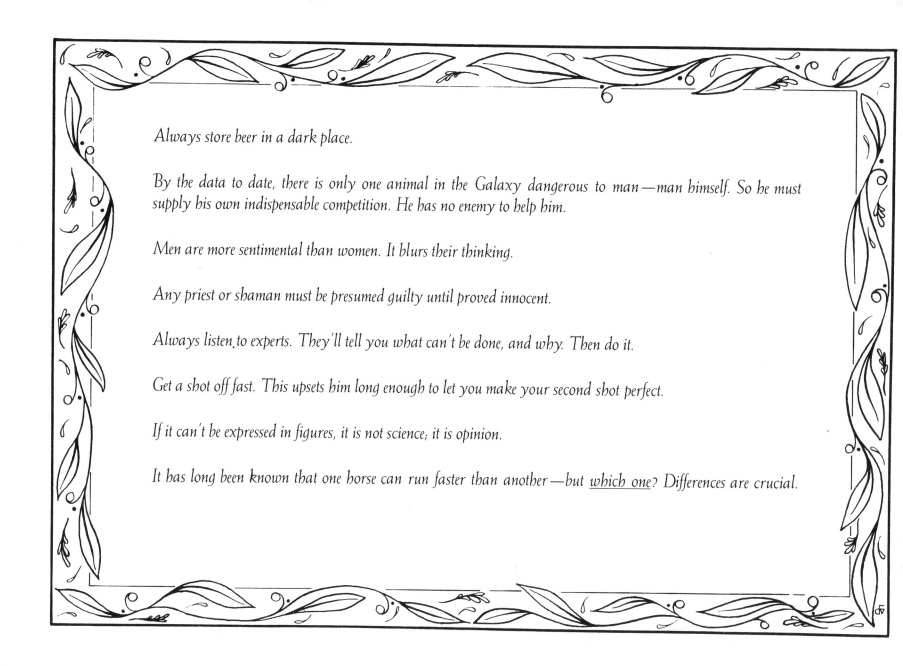

Always store beer in a dark place.

By the data to date, there is only one animal in the Galaxy dangerous to man—man himself. So he must supply his own indispensable competition. He has no enemy to help him.

Men are more sentimental than women. It blurs their thinking.

Any priest or shaman must be presumed guilty until proved innocent.

Always listen to experts. They'll tell you what can't be done, and why. Then do it.

Get a shot off fast. This upsets him long enough to let you make your second shot perfect.

If it can't be expressed in figures, it is not science; it is opinion.

It has long been known that one horse can run faster than another—but <u>which one</u>? Differences are crucial.

Certainly the game
is rigged
Don't let that stop
you; if you don't bet
you can't win.

A fake fortuneteller can be tolerated. But an authentic soothsayer should be shot on sight. Cassandra did not get half the kicking around she deserved.

Most "scientists" are bottle washers and button sorters.

If you don't like yourself, you can't like other people.

Your enemy is never a villain in his own eyes. Keep this in mind; it may offer a way to make him your friend. If not, you can kill him without hate—and quickly.

A motion to adjourn is always in order.

No state has an inherent right to survive through conscript troops and in the long run, no state ever has. Roman matrons used to say to their sons: "Come back with your shield, or on it." Later on, this custom declined. So did Rome.

Of all the strange "crimes" that human beings have legislated out of nothing, "blasphemy" is the most amazing —with "obscenity" and "indecent exposure" fighting it out for second and third place.

THERE is no conclusive evidence of life after death ~ But there is no evidence of any sort against it ~ Soon enough you will know ~

So why fret about it?

Cheops' Law: Nothing _ever_ gets built on schedule or within budget.

It is better to copulate than never.

All societies are based on rules to protect pregnant women and young children. All else is surplusage, excrescence, adornment, luxury, or folly which can—and must—be dumped in emergency to preserve this prime function. As racial survival is the only universal morality, no other basic is possible. Attempts to formulate a "perfect society" on any foundation other than "Women and children first!" is not only witless, it is automatically genocidal. Nevertheless, starry-eyed idealists (all of them male) have tried endlessly—and no doubt will keep on trying.

All men are created unequal.

Money is a powerful aphrodisiac. But flowers work almost as well.

A brute kills for pleasure. A fool kills from hate.

Delusions are often functional. A mother's opinions about her children's beauty, intelligence, goodness et cetera ad nauseam, keep her from drowning them at birth.

There is only one way to console a widow. But remember the risk.

It may be better to be a live jackal than a dead lion, but it is better still to be a live lion. And usually easier.

One man's theology is another man's belly laugh.

Sex should be friendly. Otherwise stick to mechanical toys; it's more sanitary.

Men rarely (if ever) manage to dream up a god superior to themselves. Most gods have the manners and morals of a spoiled child.

Little girls, like butterflies, need no excuse.

Avoid making irrevocable decisions while tired or hungry. N.B.: Circumstances can force your hand. So think ahead!

A generation which ignores history has no past and no future

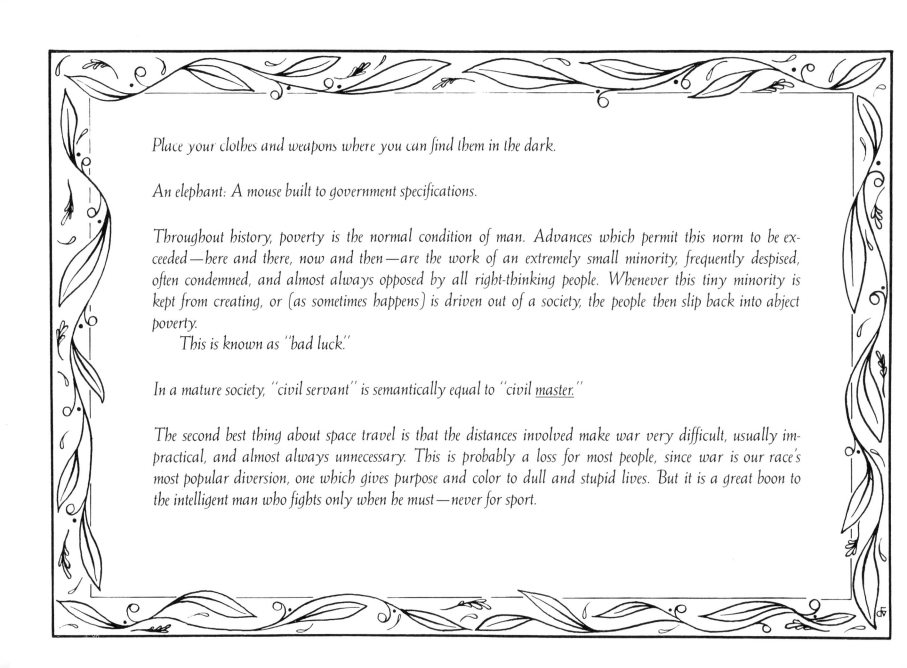

Place your clothes and weapons where you can find them in the dark.

An elephant: A mouse built to government specifications.

Throughout history, poverty is the normal condition of man. Advances which permit this norm to be exceeded—here and there, now and then—are the work of an extremely small minority, frequently despised, often condemned, and almost always opposed by all right-thinking people. Whenever this tiny minority is kept from creating, or (as sometimes happens) is driven out of a society, the people then slip back into abject poverty.

This is known as "bad luck."

In a mature society, "civil servant" is semantically equal to "civil <u>master.</u>"

The second best thing about space travel is that the distances involved make war very difficult, usually impractical, and almost always unnecessary. This is probably a loss for most people, since war is our race's most popular diversion, one which gives purpose and color to dull and stupid lives. But it is a great boon to the intelligent man who fights only when he must—never for sport.

POET who reads his verse in public may have other nasty habits.

A zygote is a gamete's way of producing more gametes. This may be the purpose of the universe.

There are hidden contradictions in the minds of people who "love Nature" while deploring the "artificialities" with which "Man has spoiled 'Nature.'" The obvious contradiction lies in their choice of words, which imply that Man and his artifacts are _not_ part of "Nature"—but beavers and their dams _are_. But the contradictions go deeper than this prima-facie absurdity. In declaring his love for a beaver dam (erected by beavers for beavers' purposes) and his hatred for dams erected by men (for the purposes of men) the "Naturist" reveals his hatred for his own race—i.e., his own self-hatred.

In the case of "Naturists" such self-hatred is understandable; they are such a sorry lot. But hatred is too strong an emotion to feel toward them; pity and contempt are the most they rate.

As for me, willy-nilly I am a man, not a beaver, and H. sapiens is the only race I have or can have. Fortunately for me, I _like_ being part of a race made up of men and women—it strikes me as a fine arrangement and perfectly "natural."

Believe it or not, there were "Naturists" who opposed the first flight to old Earth's Moon as being "unnatural" and a "despoiling of Nature."

History does not record anywhere at any time a religion that has any rational basis • Religion is a crutch for people not strong enough to stand up to the unknown without help • But, like dandruff, most people do have a religion and spend time and money on it and seem to derive considerable pleasure from fiddling with it •

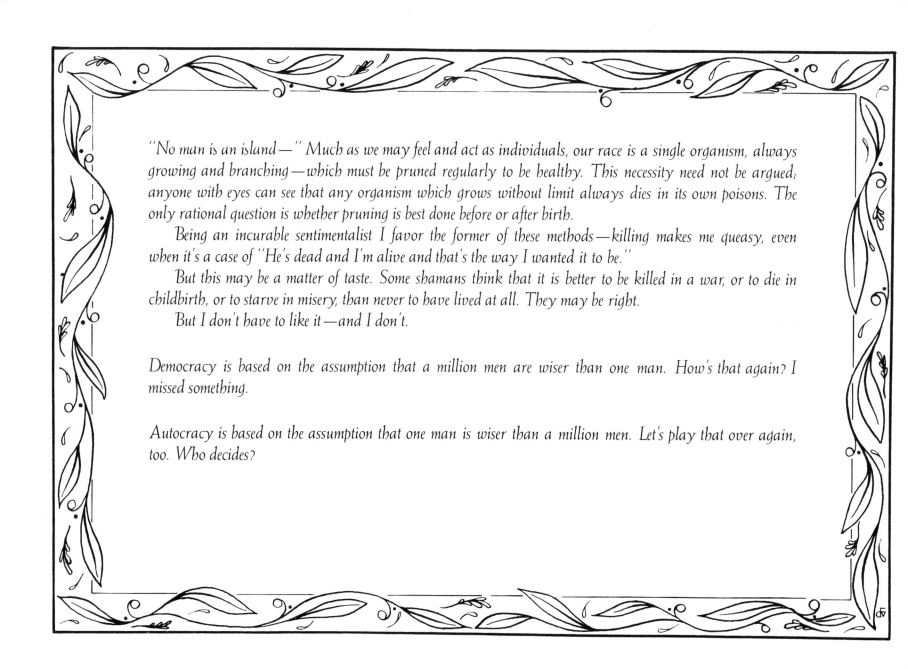

"No man is an island—" Much as we may feel and act as individuals, our race is a single organism, always growing and branching—which must be pruned regularly to be healthy. This necessity need not be argued; anyone with eyes can see that any organism which grows without limit always dies in its own poisons. The only rational question is whether pruning is best done before or after birth.

Being an incurable sentimentalist I favor the former of these methods—killing makes me queasy, even when it's a case of "He's dead and I'm alive and that's the way I wanted it to be."

But this may be a matter of taste. Some shamans think that it is better to be killed in a war, or to die in childbirth, or to starve in misery, than never to have lived at all. They may be right.

But I don't have to like it—and I don't.

Democracy is based on the assumption that a million men are wiser than one man. How's that again? I missed something.

Autocracy is based on the assumption that one man is wiser than a million men. Let's play that over again, too. Who decides?

When the need arises~and it does~you must be able to shoot your own dog. Don't farm it out~that doesn't make it nicer, it makes it worse~.

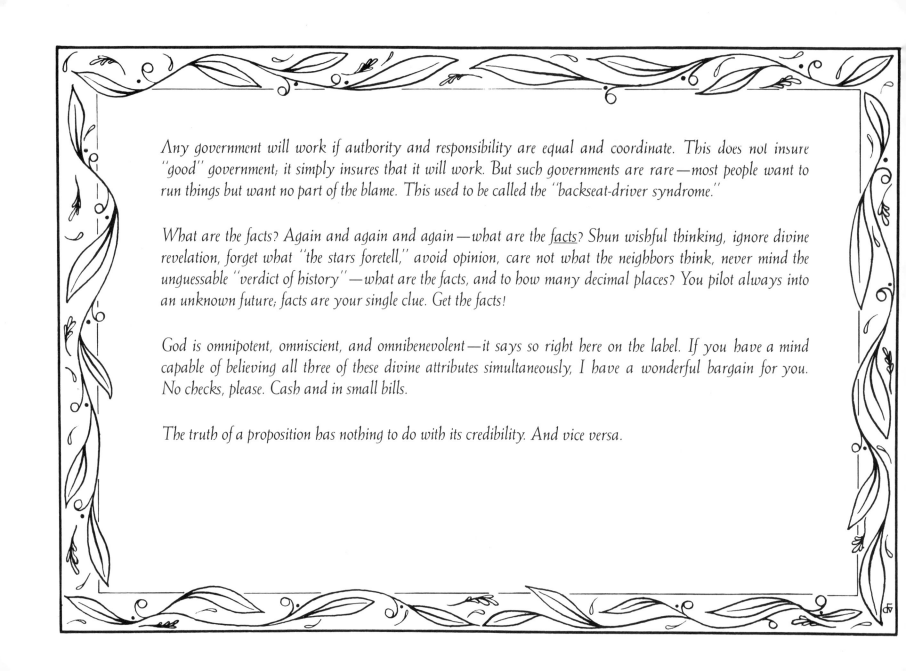

Any government will work if authority and responsibility are equal and coordinate. This does not insure "good" government; it simply insures that it will work. But such governments are rare—most people want to run things but want no part of the blame. This used to be called the "backseat-driver syndrome."

What are the facts? Again and again and again—what are the <u>facts</u>? Shun wishful thinking, ignore divine revelation, forget what "the stars foretell," avoid opinion, care not what the neighbors think, never mind the unguessable "verdict of history"—what are the facts, and to how many decimal places? You pilot always into an unknown future; facts are your single clue. Get the facts!

God is omnipotent, omniscient, and omnibenevolent—it says so right here on the label. If you have a mind capable of believing all three of these divine attributes simultaneously, I have a wonderful bargain for you. No checks, please. Cash and in small bills.

The truth of a proposition has nothing to do with its credibility. And vice versa.

Everything in excess!
To enjoy the flavor of life,
take big bites.

Moderation is for monks.

Moving parts in rubbing contact require lubrication to avoid excessive wear. Honorifics and formal politeness provide lubrication where people rub together. Often the very young, the untraveled, the naive, the unsophisticated deplore these formalities as "empty," "meaningless," or "dishonest," and scorn to use them. No matter how "pure" their motives, they thereby throw sand into machinery that does not work too well at best.

A human being should be able to change a diaper, plan an invasion, butcher a hog, conn a ship, design a building, write a sonnet, balance accounts, build a wall, set a bone, comfort the dying, take orders, give orders, cooperate, act alone, solve equations, analyze a new problem, pitch manure, program a computer, cook a tasty meal, fight efficiently, die gallantly. Specialization is for insects.

Masturbation is cheap, clean, convenient, and free of any possibility of wrongdoing—and you don't have to go home in the cold. But it's <u>lonely</u>.

Beware of altruism. It is based on self-deception, the root of all evil.

The most preposterous notion that H. sapiens has ever dreamed up is that the Lord God of Creation, Shaper and Ruler of all the Universes, wants the saccharine adoration of His creatures, can be swayed by their prayers, and becomes petulant if He does not receive this flattery. Yet this absurd fantasy, without a shred of evidence to bolster it, pays all the expenses of the oldest, largest, and least productive industry in all history.

NEVER appeal to a man's "better-nature". He may not have one. Invoking his self-interest gives you more leverage.

The second most preposterous notion is that copulation is inherently sinful.

Writing is not necessarily something to be ashamed of—but do it in private and wash your hands afterwards.

$100 placed at 7 percent interest compounded quarterly for 200 years will increase to more than $100,000,000 — by which time it will be worth nothing.

Dear, don't bore him with trivia or burden him with your past mistakes. The happiest way to deal with a man is never to tell him anything he does not need to know.

Darling, a true lady takes off her dignity with her clothes and does her whorish best. At other times you can be as modest and dignified as your <u>persona</u> requires.

If men were the automatons that behaviorists claim they are, the behaviorist psychologists could not have invented the amazing nonsense called "behaviorist psychology." So they are wrong from scratch—as clever and as wrong as phlogiston chemists.

YOU can have peace. Or you can have freedom. Don't ever count on having both at once.

The shamans are forever yacking about their snake-oil "miracles." I prefer the Real McCoy—a pregnant woman.

If the universe has any purpose more important than topping a woman you love and making a baby with her hearty help, I've never heard of it.

Thou shalt remember the Eleventh Commandment and keep it Wholly.

A touchstone to determine the actual worth of an "intellectual"—find out how he feels about astrology.

Taxes are not levied for the benefit of the taxed.

When the ship lifts, all bills are paid. No regrets.

The first time I was a drill instructor I was too inexperienced for the job—the things I taught those lads must have got some of them killed. War is too serious a matter to be taught by the inexperienced.

WHEN a place gets crowded enough to require ID's, social collapse is not far away · It is time to go elsewhere · The best thing about space travel is that it made it possible to go elsewhere ·

83m2742

A competent and self-confident person is incapable of jealousy in anything. Jealousy is invariably a symptom of neurotic insecurity.

Money is the sincerest of all flattery.
Women love to be flattered.
So do men.

You live and learn. Or you don't live long.

Peace is an extension of war by political means. Plenty of elbowroom is pleasanter—and much safer.

One man's "magic" is another man's engineering. "Supernatural" is a null word.

The phrase "we (I) (you) simply _must_—" designates something that need not be done. "That goes without saying" is a red warning. "Of course" means you had best check it yourself. These small-change clichés and others like them, when read correctly, are reliable channel markers.

Rub her feet.

A woman is not property, and husbands who think otherwise are living in a dreamworld.

If you happen to be one of the fretful minority who can do creative work, never force an idea; you'll abort it if you do. Be patient and you'll give birth to it when the time is ripe. Learn to wait.

Never crowd youngsters about their private affairs —sex especially. When they are growing up, they are nerve ends all over, and resent (quite properly) any invasion of their privacy. Oh, sure, they'll make mistakes — but that's their business, not yours. (You made your own mistakes, did you not?)

Never underestimate the power of human stupidity.

Always tell her she is beautiful, especially if she is not.

If you are part of a society that votes, then do so. There may be no candidates and no measures you want to vote <u>for</u>...but there are certain to be ones you want to vote <u>against</u>. In case of doubt, vote against. By this rule you will rarely go wrong.

    If this is too blind for your taste, consult some well-meaning fool (there is always one around) and ask his advice. Then vote the other way. This enables you to be a good citizen (if such is your wish) without spending the enormous amount of time on it that truly intelligent exercise of franchise requires.

STUPIDITY cannot be cured with money, or through education, or by legislation; Stupidity is not a sin, the victim can't help being stupid. But stupidity is the only universal capital crime; the sentence is death, there is no appeal, and execution is carried out automatically and without pity.

Sovereign ingredient for a happy marriage: Pay cash or do without. Interest charges not only eat up a household budget; awareness of debt eats up domestic felicity.

Those who refuse to support and defend a state have no claim to protection by that state. Killing an anarchist or a pacifist should not be defined as "murder" in a legalistic sense. The offense against the state, if any, should be "Using deadly weapons inside city limits," or "Creating a traffic hazard," or "Endangering bystanders," or other misdemeanor.

    However, the state may reasonably place a closed season on these exotic asocial animals whenever they are in danger of becoming extinct.

An authentic buck pacifist has rarely been seen off Earth, and it is doubtful that any have survived the trouble there...regrettable, as they had the biggest mouths and the smallest brains of any of the primates.

    The small-mouthed variety of anarchist has spread through the Galaxy at the very wave front of the Diaspora; there is no need to protect them. But they often shoot back.

Courage is the complement of fear. A man who is fearless cannot be courageous. [He is also a fool.]

Another ingredient for a happy marriage: Budget the luxuries first!

And still another—See to it that she has her own desk—then keep your hands off it!

And another—in a family argument, if it turns out you are right—apologize at once!

"God split himself into a myriad parts that he might have friends." This may not be true, but it sounds good—and is no sillier than any other theology.

To stay young requires unceasing cultivation of the ability to unlearn old falsehoods.

Does history record <u>any</u> case in which the majority was right?

When the fox gnaws—<u>smile</u>!

THE two highest achievements of the human mind are the twin concepts of "loyalty" and "duty." Whenever these twin concepts fall into disrepute ~ get out of there fast! You may possibly save yourself, but it is too late to save that society. It is doomed.

A "critic" is a man who creates nothing and thereby feels qualified to judge the work of creative men. There is logic in this; he is unbiased — he hates all creative people equally.

Money is truthful. If a man speaks of his honor, make him pay cash.

Never frighten a little man. He'll kill you.

Only a sadistic scoundrel — or a fool — tells the bald truth on social occasions.

In handling a stinging insect, move very slowly.

To be "matter of fact" about the world is to blunder into fantasy — and dull fantasy at that, as the real world is strange and wonderful.

The difference between science and the fuzzy subjects is that science requires reasoning, while those other subjects merely require scholarship.

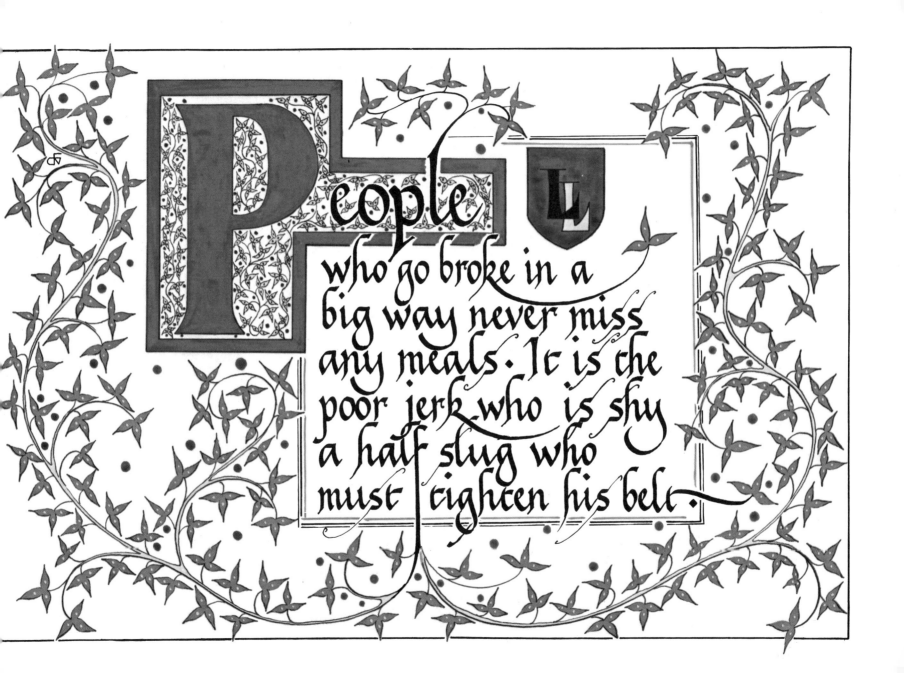

People who go broke in a big way never miss any meals. It is the poor jerk who is shy a half slug who must tighten his belt.

Copulation is spiritual in essence—or it is merely friendly exercise. On second thought, strike out "merely." Copulation is not "merely"—even when it is just a happy pastime for two strangers. But copulation at its spiritual best is so much more than physical coupling that it is different in kind as well as in degree.

The saddest feature of homosexuality is not that it is "wrong" or "sinful" or even that it can't lead to progeny—but that it is more difficult to reach through it this spiritual union. Not impossible—but the cards are stacked against it.

But—most sorrowfully—many people never achieve spiritual sharing even with the help of male-female advantage; they are condemned to wander through life alone.

Secrecy is the beginning of tyranny.

The greatest productive force is human selfishness.

Be wary of strong drink. It can make you shoot at tax collectors—and miss.

The profession of shaman has many advantages. It offers high status with a safe livelihood free of work in the dreary, sweaty sense. In most societies it offers legal privileges and immunities not granted to other men. But it is hard to see how a man who has been given a mandate from on High to spread tidings of joy to all mankind can be seriously interested in taking up a collection to pay his salary; it causes one to suspect that the shaman is on the moral level of any other con man.

But it's lovely work if you can stomach it.

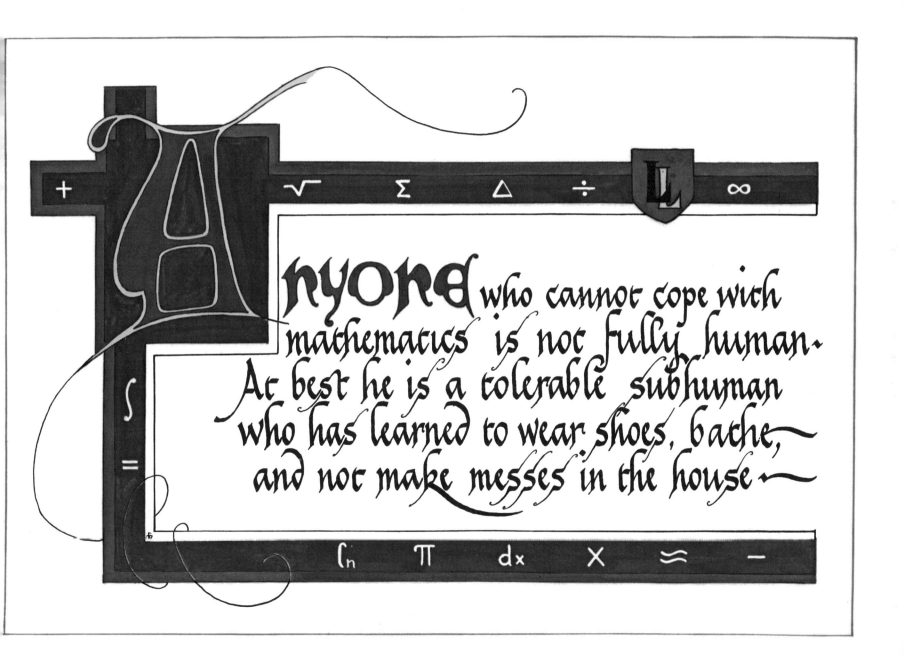

Anyone who cannot cope with mathematics is not fully human. At best he is a tolerable subhuman who has learned to wear shoes, bathe, and not make messes in the house.

A whore should be judged by the same criteria as other professionals offering services for pay—such as dentists, lawyers, hairdressers, physicians, plumbers, etc. Is she professionally competent? Does she give good measure? Is she honest with her clients?

It is possible that the percentage of honest and competent whores is higher than that of plumbers and much higher than that of lawyers. And <u>enormously</u> higher than that of professors.

Minimize your therbligs until it becomes automatic; this doubles your effective lifetime—and thereby gives time to enjoy butterflies and kittens and rainbows.

Have you noticed how much they look like orchids? Lovely!

Expertise in one field does not carry over into other fields. But experts often think so. The narrower their field of knowledge the more likely they are to think so.

Never try to outstubborn a cat.

Tilting at windmills hurts you more than the windmills.

THE

more you love, the more you can love— and the more intensely you love. Nor is there any limit on how many you can love. If a person had time enough, he could love all of that majority who are decent and just.

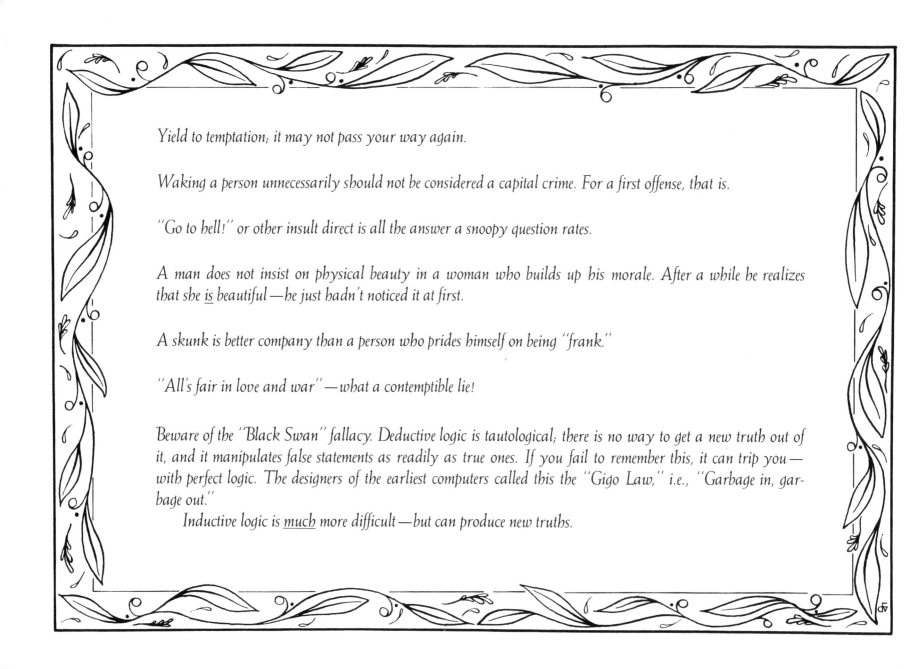

Yield to temptation; it may not pass your way again.

Waking a person unnecessarily should not be considered a capital crime. For a first offense, that is.

"Go to hell!" or other insult direct is all the answer a snoopy question rates.

A man does not insist on physical beauty in a woman who builds up his morale. After a while he realizes that she _is_ beautiful—he just hadn't noticed it at first.

A skunk is better company than a person who prides himself on being "frank."

"All's fair in love and war"—what a contemptible lie!

Beware of the "Black Swan" fallacy. Deductive logic is tautological; there is no way to get a new truth out of it, and it manipulates false statements as readily as true ones. If you fail to remember this, it can trip you—with perfect logic. The designers of the earliest computers called this the "Gigo Law," i.e., "Garbage in, garbage out."

Inductive logic is _much_ more difficult—but can produce new truths.

If tempted by something that feels "altruistic", examine your motives and root out that self-deception. Then if you still want to do it, wallow in it!

A "practical joker" deserves applause for his wit according to its quality. Bastinado is about right. For exceptional wit one might grant keelhauling. But staking him out on an anthill should be reserved for the very wittiest.

Natural laws have no pity.

On the planet Tranquille around KM849 (G-O) lives a little animal known as a "knafn." It is herbivorous and has no natural enemies and is easily approached and may be petted—sort of a six-legged puppy with scales. Stroking it is very pleasant; it wiggles its pleasure and broadcasts euphoria in some band that humans can detect. It's worth the trip.

Someday some bright boy will figure out how to record this broadcast, then some smart boy will see commercial angles—and not long after that it will be regulated and taxed.

In the meantime I have faked that name and catalog number; it is several thousand light-years off in another direction. Selfish of me—

Freedom begins when you tell Mrs. Grundy to go fly a kite.

Everybody lies about sex

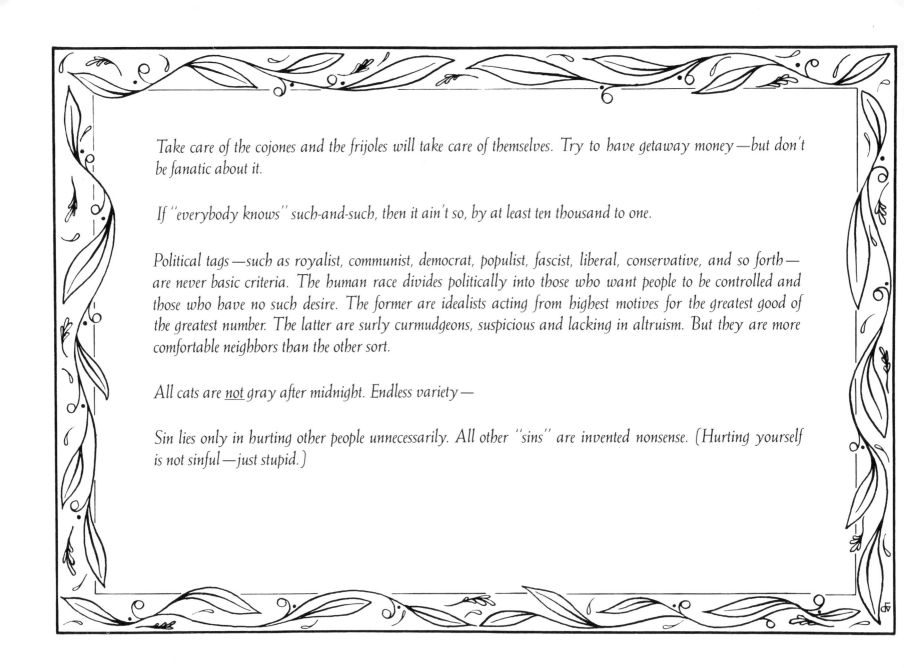

Take care of the cojones and the frijoles will take care of themselves. Try to have getaway money—but don't be fanatic about it.

If "everybody knows" such-and-such, then it ain't so, by at least ten thousand to one.

Political tags—such as royalist, communist, democrat, populist, fascist, liberal, conservative, and so forth—are never basic criteria. The human race divides politically into those who want people to be controlled and those who have no such desire. The former are idealists acting from highest motives for the greatest good of the greatest number. The latter are surly curmudgeons, suspicious and lacking in altruism. But they are more comfortable neighbors than the other sort.

All cats are _not_ gray after midnight. Endless variety—

Sin lies only in hurting other people unnecessarily. All other "sins" are invented nonsense. (Hurting yourself is not sinful—just stupid.)

There is no such thing as "social gambling": Either you are there to cut the other bloke's heart out and eat it — or you're a sucker. If you don't like this choice — don't gamble.

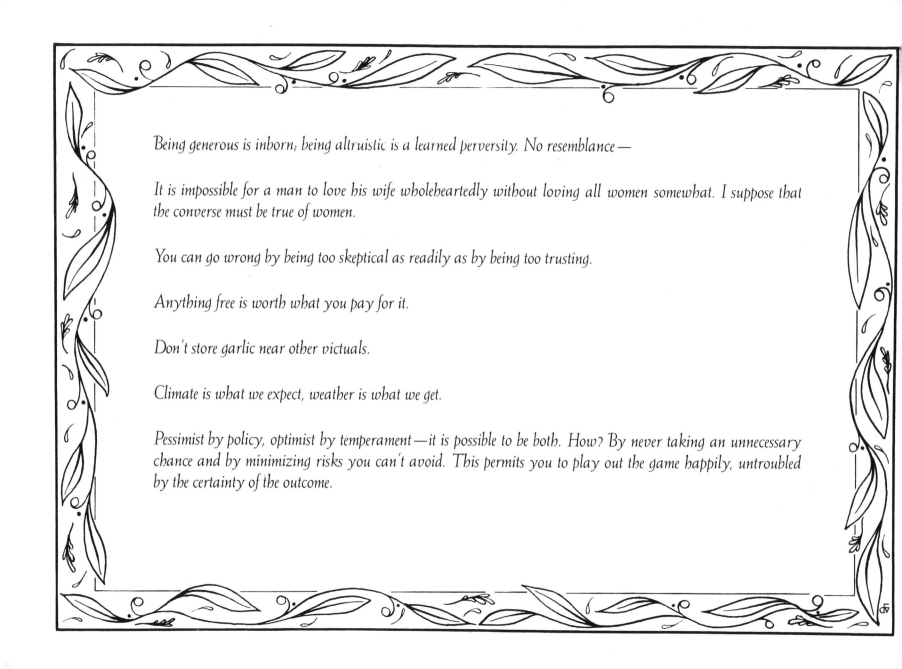

Being generous is inborn; being altruistic is a learned perversity. No resemblance—

It is impossible for a man to love his wife wholeheartedly without loving all women somewhat. I suppose that the converse must be true of women.

You can go wrong by being too skeptical as readily as by being too trusting.

Anything free is worth what you pay for it.

Don't store garlic near other victuals.

Climate is what we expect, weather is what we get.

Pessimist by policy, optimist by temperament—it is possible to be both. How? By never taking an unnecessary chance and by minimizing risks you can't avoid. This permits you to play out the game happily, untroubled by the certainty of the outcome.

A competent and self-confident person is incapable of jealousy in anything— Jealousy is invariably a symptom of neurotic insecurity.

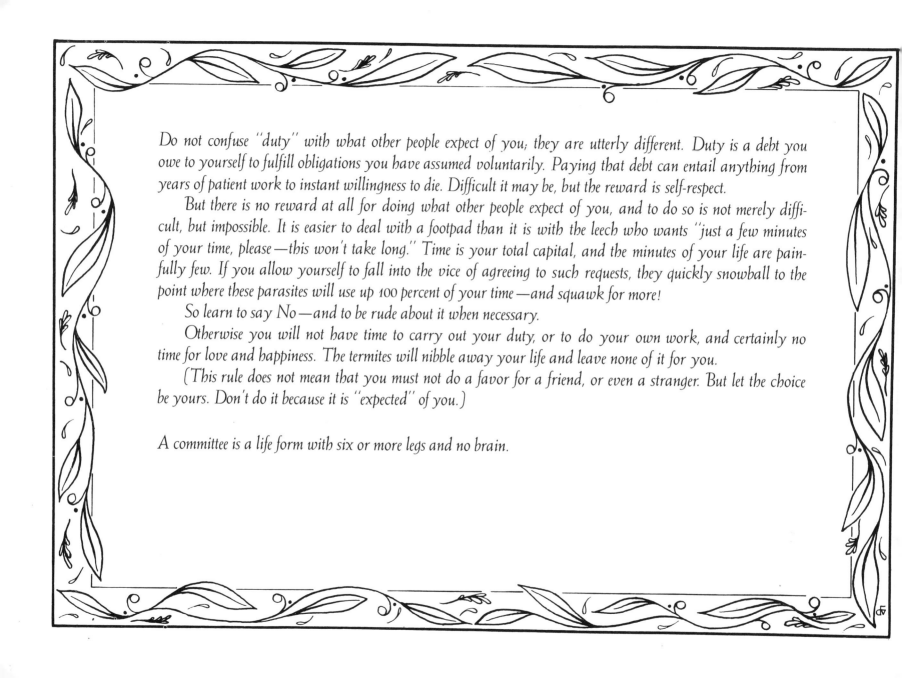

Do not confuse "duty" with what other people expect of you; they are utterly different. Duty is a debt you owe to yourself to fulfill obligations you have assumed voluntarily. Paying that debt can entail anything from years of patient work to instant willingness to die. Difficult it may be, but the reward is self-respect.

But there is no reward at all for doing what other people expect of you, and to do so is not merely difficult, but impossible. It is easier to deal with a footpad than it is with the leech who wants "just a few minutes of your time, please—this won't take long." Time is your total capital, and the minutes of your life are painfully few. If you allow yourself to fall into the vice of agreeing to such requests, they quickly snowball to the point where these parasites will use up 100 percent of your time—and squawk for more!

So learn to say No—and to be rude about it when necessary.

Otherwise you will not have time to carry out your duty, or to do your own work, and certainly no time for love and happiness. The termites will nibble away your life and leave none of it for you.

(This rule does not mean that you must not do a favor for a friend, or even a stranger. But let the choice be yours. Don't do it because it is "expected" of you.)

A committee is a life form with six or more legs and no brain.

Whenever women have insisted on absolute equality with men, they have invariably wound up with the dirty end of the stick. What they are and what they can do makes them superior to men, and their proper tactic is to demand special privileges, all the traffic will bear. They should never settle merely for equality. For women, "equality" is a disaster.

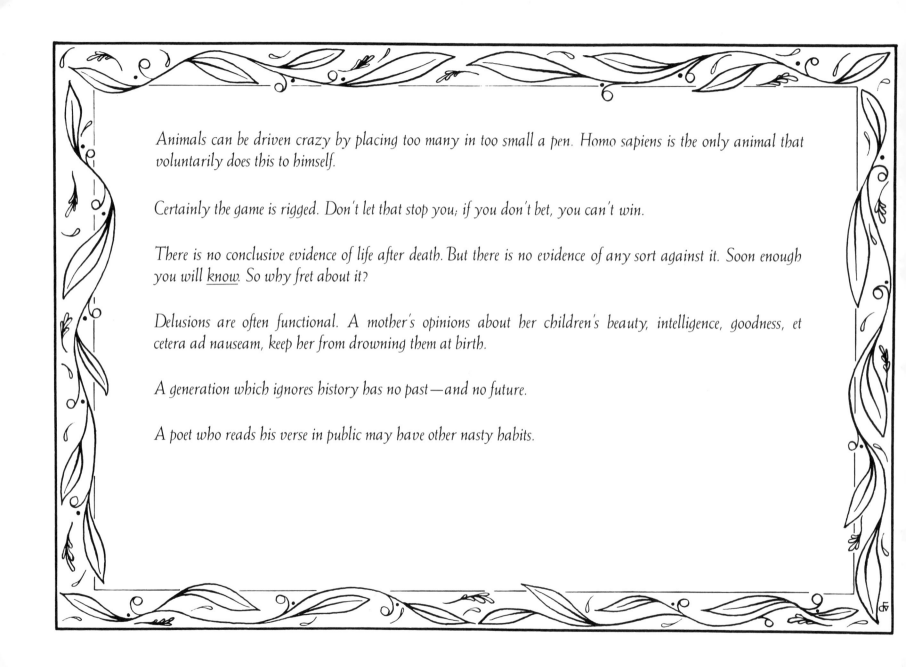

Animals can be driven crazy by placing too many in too small a pen. Homo sapiens is the only animal that voluntarily does this to himself.

Certainly the game is rigged. Don't let that stop you; if you don't bet, you can't win.

There is no conclusive evidence of life after death. But there is no evidence of any sort against it. Soon enough you will <u>know</u>. So why fret about it?

Delusions are often functional. A mother's opinions about her children's beauty, intelligence, goodness, et cetera ad nauseam, keep her from drowning them at birth.

A generation which ignores history has no past—and no future.

A poet who reads his verse in public may have other nasty habits.

Do not handicap your children by making their lives easy.

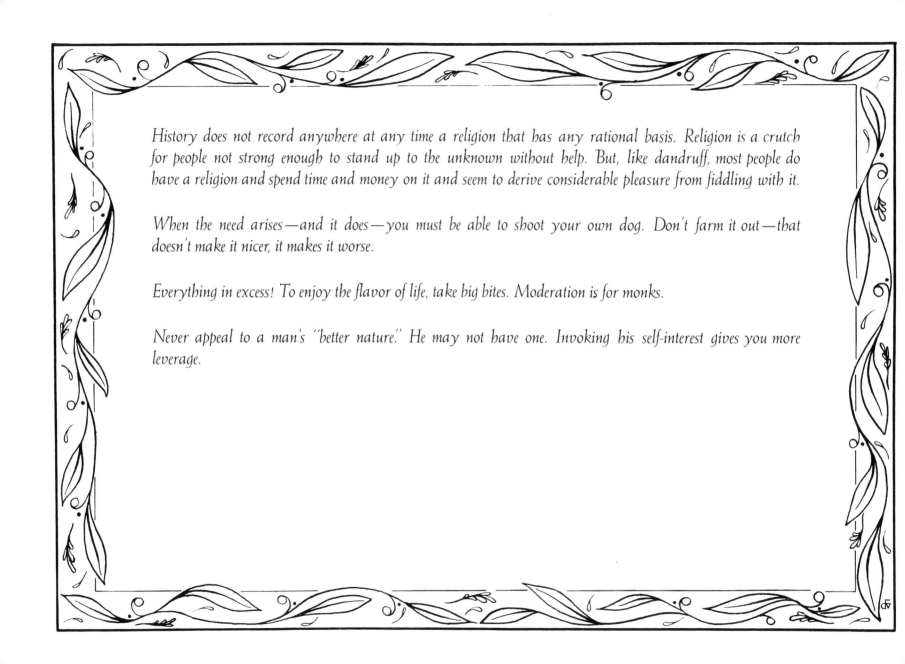

History does not record anywhere at any time a religion that has any rational basis. Religion is a crutch for people not strong enough to stand up to the unknown without help. But, like dandruff, most people do have a religion and spend time and money on it and seem to derive considerable pleasure from fiddling with it.

When the need arises—and it does—you must be able to shoot your own dog. Don't farm it out—that doesn't make it nicer, it makes it worse.

Everything in excess! To enjoy the flavor of life, take big bites. Moderation is for monks.

Never appeal to a man's "better nature." He may not have one. Invoking his self-interest gives you more leverage.

This sad little lizard told me that he was a brontosaurus on his mother's side. I did not laugh; people who boast of ancestry often have little else to sustain them. Humoring them costs nothing and adds to happiness in a world in which happiness is in short supply.

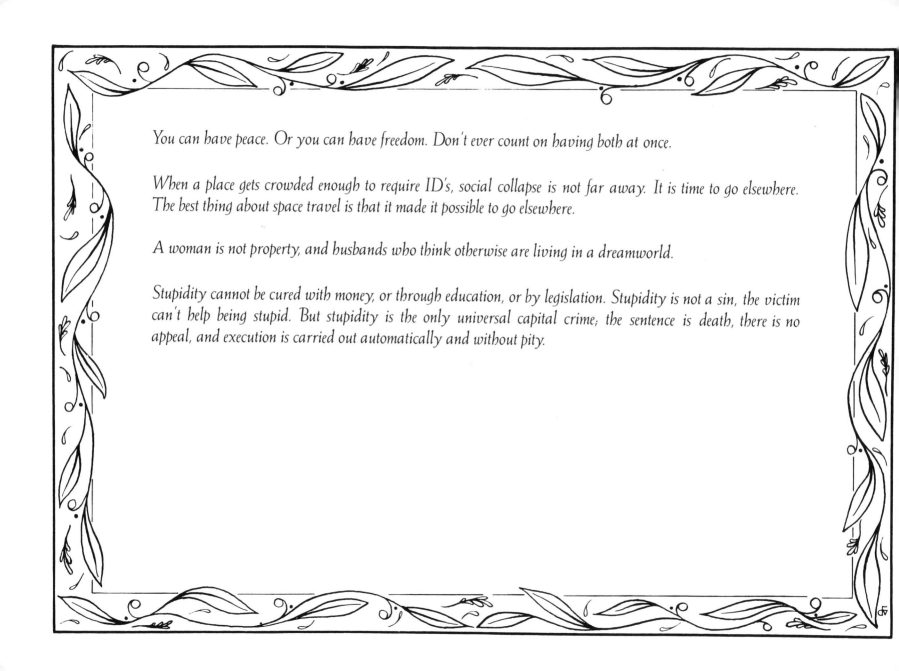

You can have peace. Or you can have freedom. Don't ever count on having both at once.

When a place gets crowded enough to require ID's, social collapse is not far away. It is time to go elsewhere. The best thing about space travel is that it made it possible to go elsewhere.

A woman is not property, and husbands who think otherwise are living in a dreamworld.

Stupidity cannot be cured with money, or through education, or by legislation. Stupidity is not a sin, the victim can't help being stupid. But stupidity is the only universal capital crime; the sentence is death, there is no appeal, and execution is carried out automatically and without pity.

Touch is the most fundamental sense. A baby experiences it, all over, before he is born and long before he learns to use sight, hearing, or taste, and no human ever ceases to need it — Keep your children short on pocket money — but long on hugs.

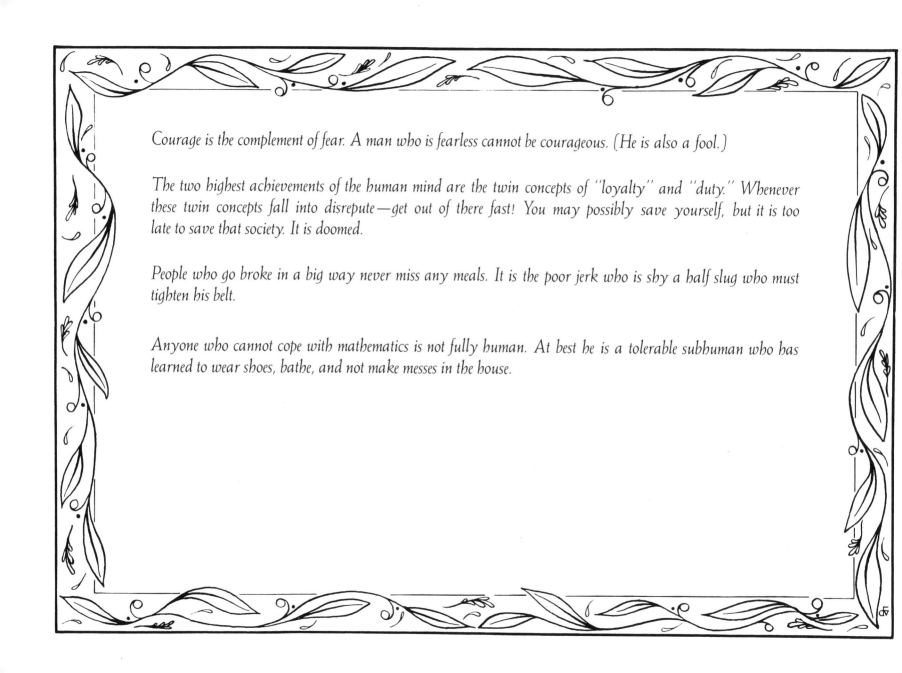

Courage is the complement of fear. A man who is fearless cannot be courageous. (He is also a fool.)

The two highest achievements of the human mind are the twin concepts of "loyalty" and "duty." Whenever these twin concepts fall into disrepute—get out of there fast! You may possibly save yourself, but it is too late to save that society. It is doomed.

People who go broke in a big way never miss any meals. It is the poor jerk who is shy a half slug who must tighten his belt.

Anyone who cannot cope with mathematics is not fully human. At best he is a tolerable subhuman who has learned to wear shoes, bathe, and not make messes in the house.

The correct way to punctuate a sentence that starts : "Of course it is none of my business but—" is to place a period after the word "but". Don't use excessive force in supplying such moron with a period. Cutting his throat is only a momentary pleasure and is bound to get you talked about—.

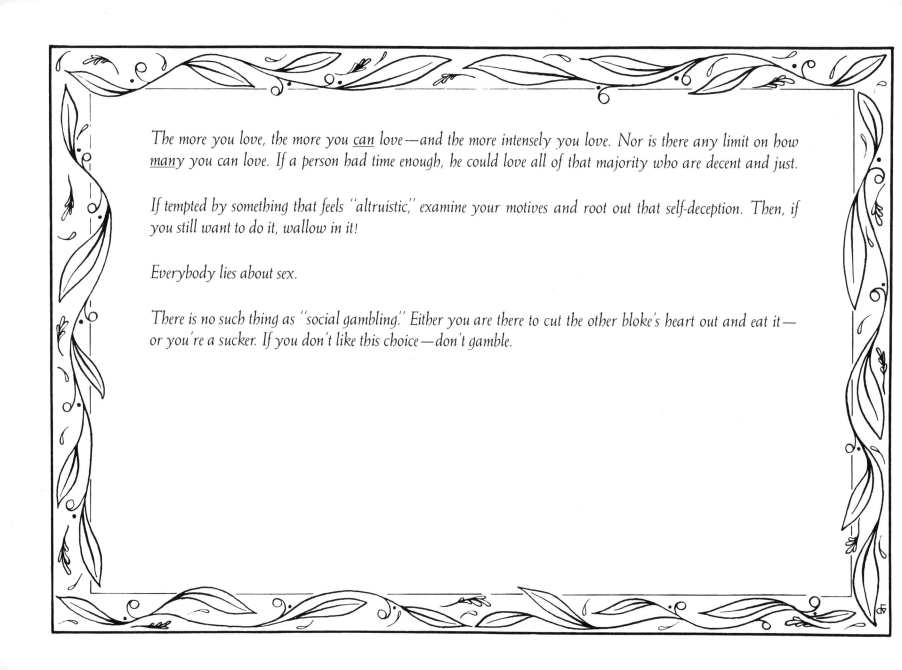

The more you love, the more you _can_ love—and the more intensely you love. Nor is there any limit on how _many_ you can love. If a person had time enough, he could love all of that majority who are decent and just.

If tempted by something that feels "altruistic," examine your motives and root out that self-deception. Then, if you still want to do it, wallow in it!

Everybody lies about sex.

There is no such thing as "social gambling." Either you are there to cut the other bloke's heart out and eat it— or you're a sucker. If you don't like this choice—don't gamble.

"I CAME, I SAW, SHE CONQUERED"

(The original Latin seems to have been garbled.)

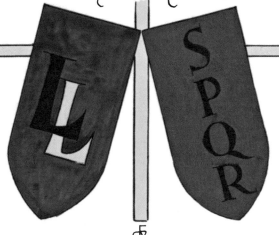

Whenever women have insisted on absolute equality with men, they have invariably wound up with the dirty end of the stick. What they are and what they can do makes them superior to men, and their proper tactic is to demand special privileges, all the traffic will bear. They should never settle merely for equality. For women, "equality" is a disaster.

Do not handicap your children by making their lives easy.

This sad little lizard told me that he was a brontosaurus on his mother's side. I did not laugh; people who boast of ancestry often have little else to sustain them. Humoring them costs nothing and adds to happiness in a world in which happiness is always in short supply.

Formal courtesy between husband and wife is even more important than it is between strangers.

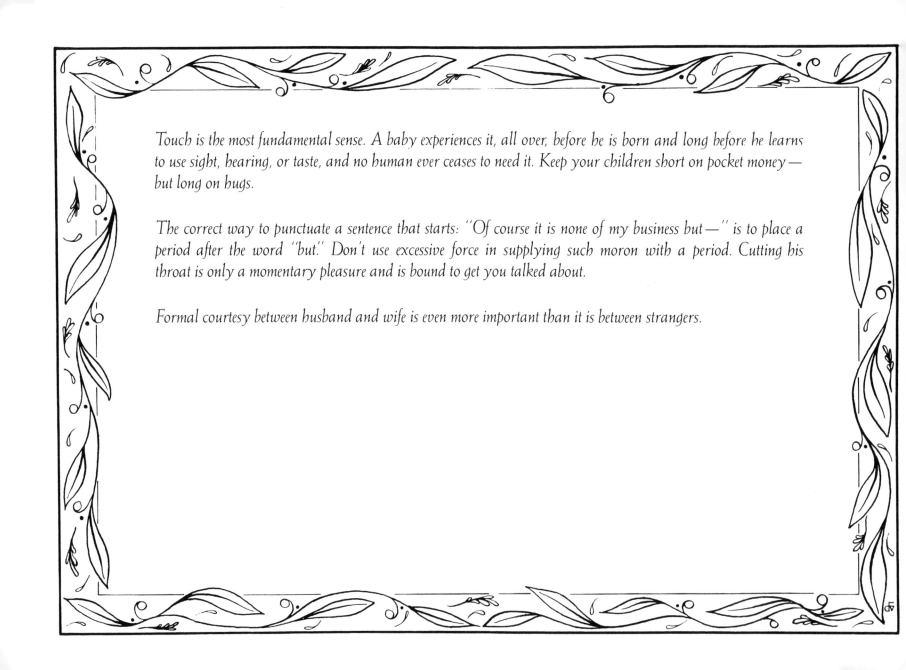

Touch is the most fundamental sense. A baby experiences it, all over, before he is born and long before he learns to use sight, hearing, or taste, and no human ever ceases to need it. Keep your children short on pocket money — but long on hugs.

The correct way to punctuate a sentence that starts: "Of course it is none of my business but —" is to place a period after the word "but." Don't use excessive force in supplying such moron with a period. Cutting his throat is only a momentary pleasure and is bound to get you talked about.

Formal courtesy between husband and wife is even more important than it is between strangers.

Don't try to have the last word.
You might get it.